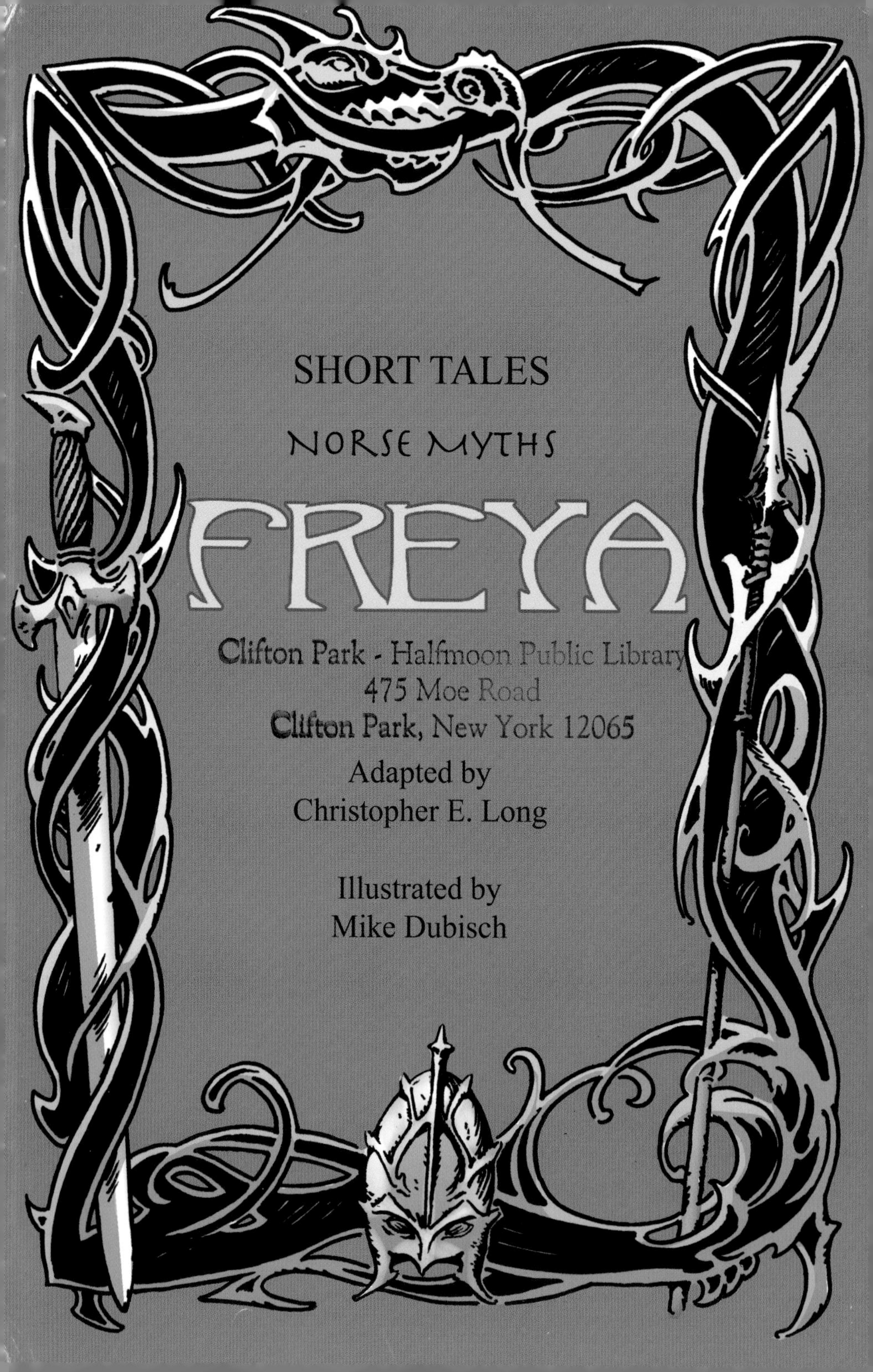

SHORT TALES

NORSE MYTHS

FREYA

Adapted by
Christopher E. Long

Illustrated by
Mike Dubisch

visit us at www.abdopublishing.com

Published by Magic Wagon, a division of the ABDO Publishing Group, 8000 West 78th Street, Edina, Minnesota, 55439.

Printed in the United States of America, North Mankato, Minnesota.
032010
092010
This book contains at least 10% recycled materials.

Adapted Text by Christopher E. Long
Illustrations by Mike Dubisch
Colors by Robby Bevard
Edited by Stephanie Hedlund
Interior Layout by Kristen Fitzner Denton
Book Design and Packaging by Shannon Eric Denton

Library of Congress Cataloging-in-Publication Data

Long, Christopher E.
Freya / adapted by Christopher E. Long ; illustrated by Mike Dubisch.
p. cm. -- (Short tales. Myths)
ISBN 978-1-60270-565-4
1. Freya (Norse deity)--Juvenile literature. 2. Goddesses, Norse--Juvenile literature. I. Dubisch, Michael. II. Title.
BL870.F48L66 2009
398.209363'01--dc22

2008032343

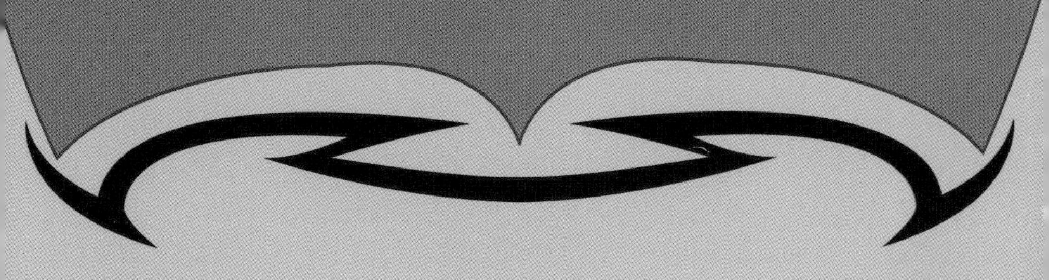

THE NORSE GODS
ODIN: The All-Father of the Gods
FRIGGA: Queen of the Gods
BALDUR: The Best Loved of the Gods
FORSETI: God of Justice
HEIMDALL: The Guardian of Asgard
HOD: God of Winter
THOR: God of Thunder
TYR: God of War
HERMOD: Messenger of the Gods
FREYR: God of Weather
LOKI: The Trickster
FREYA: Goddess of Beauty and Love

Mythical Beginnings

Freya, the Norse goddess of beauty and love, was also a skilled warrior. She became the Queen of the Valkyries, the warrior goddess who served Odin.

Freya was so powerful that she was allowed to take half of the slain warriors' souls. She gathered these souls and took them to her palace. The remaining souls went with Odin to Valhalla.

The myth of what happened to the love of Freya's life continues to be told today…

Before humankind walked the earth, Norse gods ruled the heavens. Of all these gods, the most beautiful was Freya.

Freya was a skilled warrior. She was also the queen of the Valkyries. These goddesses had a special job. They collected the souls of fallen warriors and took them to the afterlife.

Freya's beauty commanded the hearts and minds of every man. Poets wrote about her. Musicians sang her praise.

Both gods and men tried to win her heart. But none could make Freya love him.
"Freya, your beauty has captured my heart," Thor said.

But, Freya wanted a husband who loved her for what was on the inside, not on the outside.
"Men love me only for my beauty," she said.

One day, Freya was collecting souls when she spotted a mysterious figure. It was a man standing on a hill overlooking the battlefield.
"Greetings, stranger," Freya said. "Remove your hood so I might look upon your face."

"My name is Od," he said. "I'm a god."
"You are blind," Freya said, surprised.
Od laughed and said, "Yes, Freya, I am blind."

Od and Freya began to spend time together. Freya enjoyed their long walks. They told each other of their dreams, fears, and hopes. It didn't take long before their love blossomed like a flower.

"Freya, will you be my wife?" Od asked.
Freya knew her heart belonged to Od. He loved her for her, and not her beauty.
"Yes," Freya said. "I will marry you."

Odin married Freya and Od. All the gods and goddesses attended their wedding. On that day, every animal was silent and the wind didn't blow. It was the most glorious day ever.

Everyone wished them happiness and joy. Freya had never been happier. It was too good to be true.

"I've never known happiness before," Freya said. She made a silent wish that all her days would be filled with such joy.

Soon, Od had to go on a journey to the East. Freya wished her husband a speedy return.
"Nothing can tear apart true love," Od said.

Months went by, and Freya began to worry about her husband. There was no news. No one knew where he was.

Freya decided to search for Od. She grabbed her magic cloak made from falcon feathers.

The cloak gave Freya the ability to fly. She flew across the globe searching for her husband. No matter how far she flew, Freya couldn't find Od.

While flying over the sea, Freya spotted a large sea monster.

"Monster, have you seen my true love?" she asked. "I'm worried I'll never see him again."

“Freya, nothing can tear apart true love,” the sea monster growled.

"I am your husband, Od," the creature said.

"But how can that be?" Freya asked.

Od explained that Loki, the trickster, turned him into a giant sea monster.

"What shall we do now?" Freya said.
A great sorrow, like none the world had ever known, filled Freya.

Freya started to weep uncontrollably. Her true sorrow made her shed tears of pure gold.
"Freya, why are you crying?" the sea monster asked.

"You are a giant sea monster," Freya said.
"Inside, I'm still the man you fell in love with," the sea monster said.

"Love knows nothing of ugliness," the sea monster said. "If our love is true, our hearts will be together forever."

"I will love you until the end of time," Freya said. In the history of gods and men, never was there a truer love than between Freya and Od.

Many years later, Loki and his army of giants waged war on the gods. The battle was called Ragnarok. Freya fought bravely that day. Her husband fought by her side.

As the flames of Ragnarok died out, a beautiful new world was born. The old gods were gone forever, but the Norse people would always remember Freya. They honored her memory by naming a day after her, Friday!

CLIFTON PARK-HALFMOON PUBLIC LIBRARY, NY
0 00 06 03750647